‘How can the bird
that is born for
joy
Sit in a cage
and sing?’

WILLIAM BLAKE

Tyger, Tyger

Contents

MILTON

a Poem in 2 Books

To Justify the Ways of God to Men

([London:] The Author & Printer W Blake 1804)

Preface

And did those feet in ancient time
Walk upon England's mountains green;
And was the holy Lamb of God
On England's pleasant pastures seen!

And did the Countenance Divine
Shine forth upon our clouded hills?
And was Jerusalem builded here,
Among these dark Satanic Mills?

Bring me my Bow of burning gold:
Bring me my Arrows of desire:
Bring me my Spear: O clouds, unfold:
Bring me my Chariot of Fire!

I will not cease from Mental Fight,
Nor shall my Sword sleep in my hand:
Till we have built Jerusalem,
In England's green & pleasant Land.

'Would to God that all the Lord's people were Prophets.'
Numbers XI Ch 29 v.

'I saw a chapel all of gold'

I saw a chapel all of gold
That none did dare to enter in
And many weeping stood without
Weeping, mourning, worshipping.

I saw a serpent rise between
The white pillars of the door
And he forcd & forcd & forcd
Down the golden hinges tore

And along the pavement sweet
Set with pearls & rubies bright
All his slimy length he drew
Till upon the altar white

Vomiting his poisons out
On the bread & on the wine.
So I turnd into a sty
And laid me down among the swine.

‘“I die I die” the Mother said’

‘I die I die’ the Mother said,
‘My Children will die for lack of bread!
What more has the merciless tyrant said?’
The Monk sat down on her stony bed.

His Eye was dry, no tear could flow.
A hollow groan first spoke his woe.
He trembled & shudderd upon the bed.
At length with a feeble cry he said

‘When God commanded this hand to write
In the studious hours of deep midnight
He told me that All I wrote should prove
The bane of all that on Earth I love.

‘My brother starvd between two walls,
His children’s cry my soul appalls.
I mockd at the wrack & griding chain,
My bent body mocks at their torturing pain.

‘Thy father drew his sword in the north,
With his thousands strong he is marched forth.
Thy brother has armed himself in steel
To revenge the wrongs thy Children feel.

‘But vain the sword & vain the bow,
They never can work war’s overthrow!
The Hermit’s prayer & the widow’s tear
Alone can free the world from fear.’

William Blake

The hand of vengeance sought the bed
To which the purple tyrant fled.
The iron hand crushd the tyrant's head
And became a tyrant in his stead.

Songs of Innocence and of Experience

Shewing the Two Contrary States of the Human Soul

Songs of Innocence

([London:] The Author & Printer W Blake 1789)

Introduction

Piping down the valleys wild,
Piping songs of pleasant glee
On a cloud I saw a child,
And he laughing said to me:

'Pipe a song about a Lamb:'
So I piped with merry chear.
'Piper pipe that song again;'
So I piped, he wept to hear.

'Drop thy pipe, thy happy pipe;
Sing thy songs of happy chear.'
So I sung the same again,
While he wept with joy to hear.

'Piper, sit thee down and write
In a book that all may read.'
So he vanish'd from my sight
And I pluck'd a hollow reed

And I made a rural pen,
And I stain'd the water clear,
And I wrote my happy songs
Every child may joy to hear.

The Shepherd

How sweet is the Shepherd's sweet lot!
From the morn to the evening he strays;
He shall follow his sheep all the day
And his tongue shall be filled with praise.

For he hears the lamb's innocent call,
And he hears the ewe's tender reply.
He is watchful while they are in peace,
For they know when their Shepherd is nigh.

The Ecchoing Green

The Sun does arise,
And make happy the skies.
The merry bells ring
To welcome the Spring.
The sky-lark and thrush,
The birds of the bush,
Sing louder around,
To the bells' chearful sound,

While our sports shall be seen
On the Ecchoing Green.

Old John with white hair
Does laugh away care,
Sitting under the oak,
Among the old folk.
They laugh at our play,
And soon they all say:
'Such such were the joys
When we all girls & boys,
In our youth-time were seen
On the Ecchoing Green.'

Till the little ones weary
No more can be merry;
The sun does descend,
And our sports have an end:
Round the laps of their mothers
Many sisters and brothers,
Like birds in their nest,
Are ready for rest:
And sport no more seen,
On the darkening Green.

The Lamb

Little Lamb, who made thee?
Does thou know who made thee?
Gave thee life & bid thee feed

By the stream & o'er the mead;
Gave thee clothing of delight,
Softest clothing wooly bright;
Gave thee such a tender voice,
Making all the vales rejoice;
Little Lamb, who made thee?
Dost thou know who made thee?

Little Lamb, I'll tell thee,
Little Lamb, I'll tell thee:
He is called by thy name,
For he calls himself a Lamb:
He is meek & he is mild,
He became a little child:
I a child & thou a lamb,
We are called by his name.
Little Lamb, God bless thee.
Little Lamb, God bless thee.

The Little Black Boy

My mother bore me in the southern wild,
And I am black, but O! my soul is white.
White as an angel is the English child:
But I am black as if bereav'd of light.

My mother taught me underneath a tree
And sitting down before the heat of day
She took me on her lap and kissed me
And pointing to the east began to say:

'Look on the rising sun! there God does live
And gives his light and gives his heat away;
And flowers and trees and beasts and men receive
Comfort in morning, joy in the noon day.

'And we are put on earth a little space,
That we may learn to bear the beams of love;
And these black bodies and this sun-burnt face
Is but a cloud, and like a shady grove.

'For when our souls have learn'd the heat to bear
The cloud will vanish; we shall hear his voice
Saying: "come out from the grove my love & care
And round my golden tent like lambs rejoice."'

Thus did my mother say and kissed me,
And thus I say to little English boy:
When I from black and he from white cloud free,
And round the tent of God like lambs we joy:

I'll shade him from the heat till he can bear
To lean in joy upon our father's knee
And then I'll stand and stroke his silver hair
And be like him and he will then love me.

The Blossom

Merry Merry Sparrow
Under leaves so green
A happy Blossom

Sees you swift as arrow
Seek your cradle narrow
Near my Bosom.

Pretty Pretty Robin
Under leaves so green
A happy Blossom
Hears you sobbing sobbing
Pretty Pretty Robin
Near my Bosom.

The Chimney Sweeper

When my mother died I was very young,
And my father sold me while yet my tongue
Could scarcely cry 'weep weep weep weep,'
So your chimneys I sweep & in soot I sleep.

There's little Tom Dacre, who cried when his head
That curl'd like a lamb's back was shav'd, so I said:
'Hush Tom, never mind it, for when your head's bare,
You know that the soot cannot spoil your white hair.'

And so he was quiet, & that very night,
As Tom was asleeping he had such a sight,
That thousands of sweepers, Dick, Joe, Ned & Jack
Were all of them lock'd up in coffins of black,

And by came an Angel who had a bright key,
And he open'd the coffins & set them all free.
Then down a green plain leaping laughing they run
And wash in a river and shine in the Sun.

Then naked & white, all their bags left behind,
They rise upon clouds, and sport in the wind.
And the Angel told Tom if he'd be a good boy,
He'd have God for his father & never want joy.

And so Tom awoke and we rose in the dark
And got with our bags & our brushes to work.
Tho' the morning was cold, Tom was happy & warm.
So if all do their duty, they need not fear harm.

The Little Boy lost

'Father, father, where are you going?
O do not walk so fast.
Speak, father, speak to your little boy
Or else I shall be lost.'

The night was dark, no father was there;
The child was wet with dew.
The mire was deep, & the child did weep
And away the vapour flew.

The Little Boy found

The little boy lost in the lonely fen,
Led by the wand'ring light,
Began to cry, but God ever nigh,
Appeard like his father in white.

He kissed the child & by the hand led
And to his mother brought,
Who in sorrow pale thro' the lonely dale
Her little boy weeping sought.

Laughing Song

When the green woods laugh with the voice of joy
And the dimpling stream runs laughing by,
When the air does laugh with our merry wit,
And the green hill laughs with the noise of it,

When the meadows laugh with lively green
And the grasshopper laughs in the merry scene,
When Mary and Susan and Emily
With their sweet round mouths sing 'Ha, Ha, He,'

When the painted birds laugh in the shade
Where our table with cherries and nuts is spread,
Come live & be merry and join with me,
To sing the sweet chorus of 'Ha, Ha, He.'

A Cradle Song

Sweet dreams form a shade
O'er my lovely infant's head.
Sweet dreams of pleasant streams,
By happy silent moony beams.

Sweet sleep with soft down
Weave thy brows an infant crown.
Sweet sleep Angel mild,
Hover o'er my happy child.

Sweet smiles in the night,
Hover over my delight
Sweet smiles, Mother's smiles
All the livelong night beguiles.

Sweet moans, dovelike sighs,
Chase not slumber from thy eyes.
Sweet moans, sweeter smiles,
All the dovelike moans beguiles.

Sleep, sleep, happy child.
All creation slept and smil'd.
Sleep, sleep, happy sleep,
While o'er thee thy mother weep.

Sweet babe, in thy face,
Holy image I can trace.
Sweet babe, once like thee
Thy maker lay and wept for me,

Wept for me, for thee, for all,
When he was an infant small.
Thou his image ever see,
Heavenly face that smiles on thee,

Smiles on thee, on me, on all,
Who became an infant small.
Infant smiles are his own smiles;
Heaven & earth to peace beguiles.

The Divine Image

To Mercy, Pity, Peace and Love
All pray in their distress:
And to these virtues of delight
Return their thankfulness.

For Mercy, Pity, Peace and Love
Is God our father dear:
And Mercy, Pity, Peace and Love
Is Man his child and care.

For Mercy has a human heart,
Pity a human face:
And Love, the human form divine,
And Peace, the human dress.

Then every man of every clime,
That prays in his distress,
Prays to the human form divine
Love, Mercy, Pity, Peace.

And all must love the human form,
In heathen, turk or jew.
Where Mercy, Love & Pity dwell
There God is dwelling too.

Holy Thursday

Twas on a Holy Thursday, their innocent faces clean,
The children walking two & two in red & blue & green;
Grey headed beadles walkd before with wands as white as snow
Till into the high dome of Paul's they like Thames waters flow.

O what a multitude they seemd these flowers of London town!
Seated in companies they sit, with radiance all their own.
The hum of multitudes was there but multitudes of lambs,
Thousands of little boys & girls raising their innocent hands.

Now like a mighty wind they raise to heaven the voice of song,
Or like harmonious thunderings the seats of heaven among.
Beneath them sit the aged men, wise guardians of the poor;
Then cherish pity, lest you drive an angel from your door.

Night

The sun descending in the west,
The evening star does shine.
The birds are silent in their nest,
And I must seek for mine,
The moon like a flower
In heaven's high bower;
With silent delight
Sits and smiles on the night.

Farewell green fields and happy groves,
Where flocks have took delight;
Where lambs have nibbled, silent moves
The feet of angels bright;
Unseen they pour blessing,
And joy without ceasing,
On each bud and blossom,
And each sleeping bosom.

They look in every thoughtless nest,
Where birds are coverd warm;
They visit caves of every beast
To keep them all from harm:
If they see any weeping
That should have been sleeping
They pour sleep on their head
And sit down by their bed.

When wolves and tygers howl for prey
They pitying stand and weep;
Seeking to drive their thirst away,
And keep them from the sheep.
But if they rush dreadful,
The angels most heedful
Recieve each mild spirit
New worlds to inherit.

And there the lion's ruddy eyes
Shall flow with tears of gold:
And pitying the tender cries,
And walking round the fold:
Saying: 'Wrath by his meekness
And by his health sickness,
Is driven away
From our immortal day.

'And now beside thee, bleating lamb,
I can lie down and sleep;
Or think on him who bore thy name,

Graze after thee and weep.
For wash'd in life's river,
My bright mane for ever
Shall shine like the gold,
As I guard o'er the fold.'

SPRING

Sound the Flute!
Now it's mute.
Birds delight
Day and Night.
Nightingale
In the dale,
Lark in Sky
Merrily
Merrily Merrily to welcome in the Year.

Little Boy
Full of joy;
Little Girl
Sweet and small;
Cock does crow,
So do you.
Merry voice,
Infant noise,
Merrily Merrily to welcome in the Year.

Little Lamb,
Here I am;
Come and lick
My white neck.
Let me pull
Your soft Wool.
Let me kiss
Your soft face,
Merrily Merrily we welcome in the Year.

Nurse's Song

When the voices of children are heard on the green
And laughing is heard on the hill,
My heart is at rest within my breast
And everything else is still.

'Then come home my children, the sun is gone down
And the dews of night arise;
Come, come, leave off play and let us away
Till the morning appears in the skies.'

'No no, let us play, for it is yet day
And we cannot go to sleep;
Besides in the sky, the little birds fly
And the hills are all coverd with sheep.'

'Well well go & play till the light fades away
And then go home to bed.'
The little ones leaped & shouted & laugh'd
And all the hills ecchoed.

Infant Joy

'I have no name;
I am but two days old.'
What shall I call thee?
'I happy am,
Joy is my name,'
Sweet joy befall thee!

Pretty joy!
Sweet joy but two days old,
Sweet joy I call thee;
Thou dost smile,
I sing the while,
Sweet joy befall thee.

A Dream

Once a dream did weave a shade
O'er my Angel-guarded bed,
That an Emmet lost its way
Where on grass methought I lay.

Troubled, wilderd and forlorn,
Dark benighted, travel-worn,
Over many a tangled spray
All heart-broke I heard her say:

'O my children! do they cry?
Do they hear their father sigh?
Now they look abroad to see,
Now return and weep for me.'

Pitying I drop'd a tear:
But I saw a glow-worm near
Who replied: 'What wailing wight
Calls the watchman of the night?

'I am set to light the ground,
While the beetle goes his round:
Follow now the beetle's hum.
Little wanderer, hie thee home.'

On Another's Sorrow

Can I see another's woe,
And not be in sorrow too?
Can I see another's grief
And not seek for kind relief?

Can I see a falling tear,
And not feel my sorrow's share,
Can a father see his child
Weep, nor be with sorrow filld?

Can a mother sit and hear
An infant groan, an infant fear?
No, no, never can it be.
Never never can it be.

And can he who smiles on all
Hear the wren with sorrows small,
Hear the small birds grief & care,
Hear the woes that infants bear

And not sit beside the nest
Pouring pity in their breast;
And not sit the cradle near
Weeping tear on infant's tear;

And not sit both night & day,
Wiping all our tears away?
O! no never can it be.
Never never can it be.

He doth give his joy to all.
He becomes an infant small.
He becomes a man of woe;
He doth feel the sorrow too.

Think not thou canst sigh a sigh,
And thy maker is not by.
Think not thou canst weep a tear
And thy maker is not near.

O! he gives to us his joy,
That our grief he may destroy;
Till our grief is fled & gone
He doth sit by us and moan.

The Little Girl Lost

In futurity
I prophetic see,
That the earth from sleep
(Grave the sentence deep)

Shall arise and seek
For her maker meek:
And the desart wild
Become a garden mild.

In the southern clime,
Where the summer's prime
Never fades away,
Lovely Lyca lay.

Seven summers old
Lovely Lyca told,
She had wanderd long
Hearing wild birds' song.

'Sweet sleep come to me
Underneath this tree;
Do father, mother weep?
Where can Lyca sleep?

'Lost in desart wild
Is your little child,
How can Lyca sleep,
If her mother weep:

'If her heart does ake,
Then let Lyca wake:
If my mother sleep,
Lyca shall not weep.

'Frowning frowning night,
O'er this desart bright,
Let thy moon arise
While I close my eyes.'

Sleeping Lyca lay;
While the beasts of prey,
Come from caverns deep,
View'd the maid asleep.

The kingly lion stood
And the virgin view'd,
Then he gambold round
O'er the hallowd ground:

Leopards, tygers play,
Round her as she lay;
While the lion old
Bow'd his mane of gold,

And her bosom lick,
And upon her neck,
From his eyes of flame,
Ruby tears there came;

While the lioness
Loos'd her slender dress,
And naked they convey'd
To caves the sleeping maid.

The Little Girl Found

All the night in woe,
Lyca's parents go:
Over vallies deep
While the desarts weep.

Tired and woe-begone,
Hoarse with making moan:
Arm in arm seven days
They trac'd the desart ways.

Seven nights they sleep
Among shadows deep
And dream they see their child
Starv'd in desart wild.

Pale thro' pathless ways
The fancied image strays,
Famish'd, weeping, weak
With hollow piteous shriek.

Rising from unrest,
The trembling woman prest,
With feet of weary woe;
She could no further go.

In his arms he bore
Her arm'd with sorrow sore:
Till before their way
A couching lion lay.

Turning back was vain.
Soon his heavy mane
Bore them to the ground;
Then he stalk'd around

And smelling to his prey,
But their fears allay,
When he licks their hands:
And silent by them stands.

They look upon his eyes
Fill'd with deep surprise:
And wondering behold
A spirit arm'd in gold.

On his head a crown,
On his shoulders down
Flow'd his golden hair.
Gone was all their care.

'Follow me' he said,
'Weep not for the maid;
In my palace deep,
Lyca lies asleep.'

Then they followed
Where the vision led;
And saw their sleeping child,
Among tygers wild.

To this day they dwell
In a lonely dell
Nor fear the wolvish howl,
Nor the lions growl.

The School Boy

I love to rise in a summer morn,
When the birds sing on every tree;
The distant huntsman winds his horn,
And the sky-lark sings with me.
O! what sweet company.

But to go to school in a summer morn,
O! it drives all joy away:
Under a cruel eye outworn,
The little ones spend the day
In sighing and dismay.

Ah! then at times I drooping sit,
And spend many an anxious hour,
Nor in my book can I take delight,
Nor sit in learning's bower,
Worn thro' with the dreary shower.

How can the bird that is born for joy
Sit in a cage and sing?
How can a child when fears annoy
But droop his tender wing
And forget his youthful spring?

O! father & mother, if buds are nip'd,
And blossoms blown away,
And if the tender plants are strip'd
Of their joy in the springing day,
By sorrow and cares dismay,

How shall the summer arise in joy,
Or the summer fruits appear?
Or how shall we gather what griefs destroy
Or bless the mellowing year,
When the blasts of winter appear?

The Voice of the Ancient Bard

Youth of delight, come hither
And see the opening morn,
Image of truth new-born.
Doubt is fled & clouds of reason
Dark disputes & artful teazing.
Folly is an endless maze,
Tangled roots perplex her ways.
How many have fallen there!
They stumble all night over bones of the dead:
And feel they know not what but care;
And wish to lead others when they should be led.

Songs of Experience

([Lambeth:] The Author & Printer W. Blake, 1794)

Introduction

Hear the voice of the Bard!
Who Present, Past, & Future sees;
Whose ears have heard
The Holy Word
That walk'd among the ancient trees,

Calling the lapsed Soul
And weeping in the evening dew:
That might controll
The starry pole;
And fallen fallen light renew!

'O Earth O Earth return
Arise from out the dewy grass;
Night is worn,
And the morn
Rises from the slumberous mass.

'Turn away no more:
Why wilt thou turn away?
The starry floor,
The watry shore
Is giv'n thee till the break of day.'

Earth's Answer

Earth raisd up her head
From the darkness dread & drear.
Her light fled:
Stony dread!
And her locks cover'd with grey despair.

'Prison'd on watry shore
Starry Jealousy does keep my den;
Cold and hoar
Weeping o'er
I hear the father of the ancient men.

'Selfish father of men!
Cruel jealous selfish fear!
Can delight
Chain'd in night
The virgins of youth and morning bear?

'Does spring hide its joy
When buds and blossoms grow?
Does the sower
Sow by night
Or the plowman in darkness plow?

'Break this heavy chain
That does freeze my bones around.
Selfish! vain!
Eternal bane!
That free Love with bondage bound.'

The Clod & the Pebble

'Love seeketh not Itself to please,
Nor for itself hath any care;
But for another gives its ease,
And builds a Heaven in Hell's despair.'

So sang a little Clod of Clay,
Trodden with the cattle's feet:
But a Pebble of the brook
Warbled out these metres meet:

'Love seeketh only Self to please
To bind another to Its delight;
Joys in another's loss of ease,
And builds a Hell in Heaven's despite.'

Holy Thursday

Is this a holy thing to see,
In a rich and fruitful land,
Babes reducd to misery,
Fed with cold and usurous hand?

Is that trembling cry a song?
Can it be a song of joy?
And so many children poor?
It is a land of poverty!

And their sun does never shine,
And their fields are bleak and bare,
And their ways are fill'd with thorns:
It is eternal winter there.

For where-e'er the sun does shine,
And where-e'er the rain does fall:
Babe can never hunger there,
Nor poverty the mind appall.

The Chimney Sweeper

A little black thing among the snow:
Crying 'weep, weep,' in notes of woe!
'Where are thy father & mother? say?'
'They are both gone up to the church to pray.

'Because I was happy upon the heath,
And smil'd among the winter's snow:
They clothed me in the clothes of death,
And taught me to sing the notes of woe.

'And because I am happy & dance & sing,
They think they have done me no injury:
And are gone to praise God & his Priest & King
Who make up a heaven of our misery.'

Nurse's Song

When the voices of children are heard on the green
And whisprings are in the dale:
The days of my youth rise fresh in my mind,
My face turns green and pale.

Then come home my children, the sun is gone down
And the dews of night arise;
Your spring & your day are wasted in play
And your winter and night in disguise.

The Sick Rose

O Rose, thou art sick,
The invisible worm,
That flies in the night
In the howling storm:

Has found out thy bed
Of crimson joy:
And his dark secret love
Does thy life destroy.

The Fly

Little Fly
Thy summer's play
My thoughtless hand
Has brush'd away.

Am not I
A fly like thee?
Or art not thou
A man like me?

For I dance
And drink & sing:
Till some blind hand
Shall brush my wing.

If thought is life
And strength & breath:
And the want
Of thought is death;

Then am I
A happy fly,
If I live,
Or if I die.

The Angel

I dreamt a Dream! what can it mean?
And that I was a maiden Queen:
Guarded by an Angel mild:
Witless woe was neer beguil'd!

And I wept both night and day
And he wip'd my tears away
And I wept both day and night
And hid from him my heart's delight

So he took his wings and fled:
Then the morn blush'd rosy red:
I dried my tears & armd my fears
With ten thousand shields and spears.

Soon my Angel came again;
I was arm'd, he came in vain:
For the time of youth was fled
And grey hairs were on my head.

The Tyger

Tyger, Tyger, burning bright,
In the forests of the night:
What immortal hand or eye
Could frame thy fearful symmetry?

In what distant deeps or skies
Burnt the fire of thine eyes?
On what wings dare he aspire?
What the hand dare seize the fire?

And what shoulder, & what art,
Could twist the sinews of thy heart?
And when thy heart began to beat,
What dread hand? & what dread feet?

What the hammer? what the chain,
In what furnace was thy brain?
What the anvil? what dread grasp
Dare its deadly terrors clasp!

When the stars threw down their spears
And waterd heaven with their tears:
Did he smile his work to see?
Did he who made the Lamb make thee?

Tyger, Tyger burning bright,
In the forests of the night:
What immortal hand or eye
Dare frame thy fearful symmetry?

My Pretty Rose Tree

A flower was offerd to me;
Such a flower as May never bore,
But I said 'I've a Pretty Rose-tree,'
And I passed the sweet flower o'er.

Then I went to my Pretty Rose-tree
To tend her by day and by night,
But my Rose turnd away with jealousy
And her thorns were my only delight.

Ah! Sun Flower

Ah Sun-flower! weary of time,
Who countest the steps of the Sun:
Seeking after that sweet golden clime
Where the traveller's journey is done;

Where the Youth pined away with desire,
And the pale Virgin shrouded in snow
Arise from their graves and aspire
Where my Sun-flower wishes to go.

The Lilly

The modest Rose puts forth a thorn:
The humble Sheep a threatning horn:
While the Lilly white shall in Love delight,
Nor a thorn nor a threat stain her beauty bright.

The Garden of Love

I went to the Garden of Love,
And saw what I never had seen:
A Chapel was built in the midst,
Where I used to play on the green.

And the gates of this Chapel were shut,
And 'Thou shalt not' writ over the door;
So I turn'd to the Garden of Love,
That so many sweet flowers bore,

And I saw it was filled with graves,
And tomb-stones where flowers should be:
And Priests in black gowns were walking their rounds,
And binding with briars my joys & desires.

The Little Vagabond

Dear Mother, dear Mother, the Church is cold,
But the Ale-house is healthy & pleasant & warm:
Besides I can tell where I am used well,
Such usage in heaven will never do well.

But if at the Church they would give us some Ale,
And a pleasant fire our souls to regale:
We'd sing and we'd pray all the live-long day;
Nor ever once wish from the Church to stray.

Then the Parson might preach & drink & sing,
And we'd be as happy as birds in the spring:
And modest dame Lurch, who is always at Church
Would not have bandy children nor fasting nor birch.

And God like a father rejoicing to see
His children as pleasant and happy as he;
Would have no more quarrel with the Devil or the Barrel
But kiss him & give him both drink and apparel.

London

I wander thro' each charter'd street,
Near where the charter'd Thames does flow
And mark in every face I meet
Marks of weakness, marks of woe.

In every cry of every Man,
In every Infant's cry of fear,
In every voice; in every ban,
The mind-forg'd manacles I hear.

How the Chimney-sweeper's cry
Every blackning Church appalls,
And the hapless Soldier's sigh
Runs in blood down Palace walls

But most thro' midnight streets I hear
How the youthful Harlot's curse
Blasts the new born Infant's tear
And blights with plagues the Marriage hearse.

The Human Abstract

Pity would be no more
If we did not make somebody Poor:
And Mercy no more could be
If all were as happy as we;

And mutual fear brings peace;
Till the selfish loves increase.
Then Cruelty knits a snare,
And spreads his baits with care.

He sits down with holy fears,
And waters the ground with tears;
Then Humility takes its root
Underneath his foot.

Soon spreads the dismal shade
Of Mystery over his head;
And the Catterpiller and Fly
Feed on the Mystery.

And it bears the fruit of Deceit,
Ruddy and sweet to eat;
And the Raven his nest has made
In its thickest shade.

The Gods of the earth and sea
Sought thro' Nature to find this Tree
But their search was all in vain:
There grows one in the Human Brain.

Infant Sorrow

My mother groand! My father wept.
Into the dangerous world I leapt:
Helpless, naked, piping loud:
Like a fiend hid in a cloud.

Struggling in my father's hands:
Striving against my swadling bands:
Bound and weary I thought best
To sulk upon my mother's breast.

A Poison Tree

I was angry with my friend:
I told my wrath, my wrath did end.
I was angry with my foe:
I told it not, my wrath did grow.

And I waterd it in fears,
Night & morning with my tears:
And I sunned it with smiles,
And with soft deceitful wiles.

And it grew both day and night,
Till it bore an apple bright,
And my foe beheld it shine,
And he knew that it was mine,

And into my garden stole,
When the night had veild the pole:
In the morning glad I see
My foe outstretchd beneath the tree.

A Little Boy Lost

'Nought loves another as itself
Nor venerates another so,
Nor is it possible to Thought
A greater than itself to know:

'And Father, how can I love you,
Or any of my brothers more?
I love you like the little bird
That picks up crumbs around the door.'

The Priest saw by and heard the child,
In trembling zeal he siez'd his hair:
He led him by his little coat;
And all admir'd the Priestly care.

And standing on the altar high,
'Lo what a fiend is here!' said he:
'One who sets reason up for judge
Of our most holy Mystery.'

The weeping child could not be heard.
The weeping parents wept in vain:
They strip'd him to his little shirt
And bound him in an iron chain,

And burn'd him in a holy place,
Where many had been burn'd before:
The weeping parents wept in vain.
Are such things done on Albion's shore?

A Little Girl Lost

Children of the future Age,
Reading this indignant page;
Know that in a former time,
Love! sweet Love! was thought a crime.

In the Age of Gold,
Free from winter's cold
Youth and maiden bright
To the holy light,
Naked in the sunny beams delight.

Once a youthful pair
Fill'd with softest care
Met in garden bright,
Where the holy light
Had just removd the curtains of the night.

There in rising day
On the grass they play:
Parents were afar:
Strangers came not near:
And the maiden soon forgot her fear.

Tired with kisses sweet
They agree to meet,
When the silent sleep
Waves o'er heaven's deep:
And the weary tired wanderers weep.

To her father white
Came the maiden bright:
But his loving look,
Like the holy book,
All her tender limbs with terror shook.

'Ona! pale and weak!
To thy father speak:
O the trembling fear!
O the dismal care!
That shakes the blossoms of my hoary hair.'

To Tirzah

Whate'er is Born of Mortal Birth
Must be consumed with the Earth
To rise from Generation free:
Then what have I to do with thee?

The Sexes sprung from Shame & Pride,
Blowd in the morn; in evening died
But Mercy changd Death into Sleep;
The Sexes rose to work & weep.

Thou Mother of my Mortal part
With cruelty didst mould my Heart
And with false self-decieving tears
Didst bind my Nostrils, Eyes & Ears,

Didst close my Tongue in senseless clay
And me to Mortal Life betray:
The Death of Jesus set me free,
Then what have I to do with thee?

A Divine Image

Cruelty has a Human Heart
And Jealousy a Human Face,
Terror the Human Form Divine
And Secrecy the Human Dress.

The Human Dress is forged Iron,
The Human Form a fiery Forge,
The Human Face a Furnace seal'd,
The Human Heart its hungry Gorge.

The Ballads (or Pickering) Manuscript
([?after 1807])

The Mental Traveller

I traveld thro' a Land of Men,
A Land of Men & Women too
And heard & saw such dreadful things
As cold Earth wanderers never knew

For there the Babe is born in joy
That was begotten in dire woe
Just as we Reap in joy the fruit
Which we in bitter tears did Sow

And if the Babe is born a Boy
He's given to a Woman Old
Who nails him down upon a rock,
Catches his Shrieks in Cups of gold.

She binds iron thorns around his head,
She pierces both his hands & feet,
She cuts his heart out at his side
To make it feel both cold & heat.

Her fingers number every Nerve
Just as a Miser counts his gold;
She lives upon his shrieks & cries
And She grows young as he grows old

Till he becomes a bleeding youth
And she becomes a Virgin bright;
Then he rends up his Manacles
And binds her down for his delight.

He plants himself in all her Nerves
Just as a Husbandman his mould
And She becomes his dwelling place
And Garden fruitful Seventy fold.

An aged Shadow soon he fades
Wandring round an Earthly Cot
Full filled all with gems & gold
Which he by industry had got

And these are the gems of the Human Soul,
The rubies & pearls of a lovesick eye,
The countless gold of the akeing heart,
The martyr's groan & the lover's sigh.

They are his meat, they are his drink;
He feeds the Beggar & the Poor
And the way faring Traveller;
For ever open is his door.

His grief is their eternal joy;
They make the roofs & walls to ring
Till from the fire on the hearth
A little Female Babe does spring

And she is all of solid fire
And gems & gold that none his hand
Dares stretch to touch her Baby form
Or wrap her in his swaddling-band

But She comes to the Man she loves
If young or old or rich or poor;
They soon drive out the aged Host
A Beggar at another's door.

He wanders weeping far away
Untill some other take him in
Oft blind & age-bent, sore distrest
Until he can a Maiden win

And to allay his freezing Age
The Poor Man takes her in his arms;
The Cottage fades before his Sight,
The garden & its lovely Charms.

The Guests are scatterd thro' the land
For the Eye altering alters all;
The Senses roll themselves in fear
And the flat Earth becomes a Ball;

The Stars, Sun, Moon all shrink away
A desart vast without a bound
And nothing left to eat or drink
And a dark desart all around.

The honey of her Infant lips,
The bread & wine of her sweet smile,
The wild game of her roving Eye
Does him to Infancy beguile

For as he eats & drinks he grows
Younger & younger every day
And on the desart wild they both
Wander in terror & dismay.

Like the wild Stag she flees away,
Her fear plants many a thicket wild
While he pursues her night & day
By various arts of Love beguild,

By various arts of Love & Hate
Till the wide desart planted oer
With Labyrinths of wayward Love
Where roams the Lion, Wolf & Boar

Till he becomes a wayward Babe
And she a weeping Woman Old.
Then many a Lover wanders here;
The Sun & Stars are nearer rolld.

The tree brings forth sweet Extacy
To all who in the desart roam
Till many a City there is Built
And many a pleasant Shepherd's home

But when they find the frowning Babe
Terror strikes thro the region wide;
They cry 'the Babe, the Babe is Born'
And flee away on Every side

For who dare touch the frowning form
His arm is witherd to its root;
Lions, Boars, Wolves all howling flee
And every Tree does shed its fruit

And none can touch the frowning form
Except it be a Woman Old;
She nails him down upon the Rock
And all is done as I have told.

Penguin Little Black Classics Vol. I

01. GIOVANNI BOCCACCIO
Mrs Rosie and the Priest

02. EDGAR ALLAN POE
The Tell-Tale Heart

03. ANTON CHEKHOV
Gooseberries

04. LEO TOLSTOY
How Much Land Does a Man Need?

05. GUSTAVE FLAUBERT
A Simple Heart

06. RYUNOSUKE AKUTAGAWA
The Life of a Stupid Man

07. THOMAS HARDY
The Withered Arm

08. KENKO
A Cup of Sake Beneath the Cherry Trees

09. WILLIAM BLAKE
Tyger Tyger

10. RAINER MARIA RILKE
Letters to a Young Poet

‘She decided she would teach him to speak and he was very soon able to say, “Pretty boy!”, “Your servant, sir!” and “Hail Mary!”’

“为了欢乐而出世的鸟儿
怎能坐在笼中歌唱？”

PENGUIN

LITTLE BLACK

CLASSICS

虎！虎！

Tyger, Tyger

［英］威廉·布莱克 著

张炽恒 译

中信出版集团·北京

图书在版编目（CIP）数据

企鹅经典·小黑书.第一辑:英、汉/(日)吉田兼好等著;文东等译.-- 北京:中信出版社,2018.11(2022.7 重印)
书名原文:Penguin Little Black Classics
ISBN 978-7-5086-9400-9

Ⅰ.①企… Ⅱ.①吉… ②文… Ⅲ.①世界文学—作品综合集—英、汉 Ⅳ.①I11

中国版本图书馆 CIP 数据核字 (2018) 第 193780 号

企鹅经典：小黑书　第一辑
虎！虎！

著　　者：[英]威廉·布莱克
译　　者：张炽恒
出版发行：中信出版集团股份有限公司
（北京市朝阳区惠新东街甲 4 号富盛大厦 2 座 邮编 100029）
承 印 者：河北鹏润印刷有限公司

开　　本：787mm×1092mm　1/32　　印　　张：41　　字　　数：300 千字
版　　次：2018 年 11 月第 1 版　　印　　次：2022 年 7 月第 13 次印刷
京权图字：01-2018-6477
书　　号：ISBN 978-7-5086-9400-9
定　　价：149.00 元（全 10 册）

服务热线：400-600-8099
投稿邮箱：author@citicpub.com

目录

/ 经验之歌（*1794*）

《弥尔顿》序诗

要是远古时那些圣足
曾在英格兰的群山上徜徉；
要是那神圣的上帝的羊羔
到过英格兰的快乐的牧场！

那张神圣的脸庞可曾
照亮我们阴云中的山峦？
耶路撒冷可曾建起，在这些
昏暗的撒旦的磨坊[1]之间？

把我那灼亮的金弓带给我，
把我那愿望的箭矢带给我，
带给我长矛，招展的云彩呀！
把我那烈火的战车带给我！

我不会停止内心的战斗，
我的剑也不会在手中安眠，

1.“磨坊”一语双关，原文 mill 也指工厂。（说明：书中脚注除特别标明的之外，均为译者注。）

直到我们建立起耶路撒冷，

在英格兰青翠而快乐的地面。

我看见一座全金的教堂

我看见一座全金的教堂，
谁也没有胆量进去，
许多人悲叹着站在外面，
悲叹，哀哭，膜拜顶礼。

我看见一条巨蛇出现
在那些白色门柱中间，
他用力挤呀挤呀挤呀，
终于挤落了黄金的铰链。

沿着可爱的，铺满珍珠
以及灿灿宝石的通道，
他伸直他那黏滑的蛇身，
直伸到白色的祭坛上面。

他向外喷射出他的毒液，
喷在面包和啤酒上面，
于是我折进了一个猪圈，
躺在那些猪猡中间。

“我死了，我死了。”母亲说道

“我死了，我死了。”母亲说道，
“我的孩子们将因饥馑而亡！
那不仁的暴君还说了些什么？”
修士坐在她冰硬的床上。

他眼睛枯涩，泪已哭干，
一声长叹道破了悲伤。
他在床上瑟瑟地抖颤，
最后无力地开始哭讲：

“在勤学的深夜，当这双手
受命于上帝而写作的时候，
他说我写下的一切将证明
尘世间我所爱的一切的毒性。

“我兄弟求生无门而饿死，
他的孩子们哭得我心悸；
我嘲笑那嘎嘎响的破旧锁链，
我伛偻的身体嘲笑酷刑的熬煎。

“你父亲在北方拔出利剑，
率万千壮士奋勇向前；
你兄弟已操起钢铁的武器，
要报复你的孩子们所受的冤屈。

“但利剑和弓矢无济于我们，
它们永不能打倒战争；
唯隐士的祈祷和寡妇的泪滴
才能使这世界摆脱恐惧。”

复仇的手在那床上搜，
穿紫袍的暴君闻声逃走。
铁手捏碎了暴君的头颈，
又取而代之成了暴君。

天真之歌

(1789)

序诗

吹着笛儿，我走下野谷，
欢乐的笛声随风轻飘。
我看见云彩上有个小孩[1]，
孩子他笑着，向我说道：

“吹个歌唱小羊羔的歌！”
我兴高采烈地吹了一曲。
“再吹，再吹一次那歌儿！”
我又吹时他淌下了泪滴。

“放下笛儿，那快乐的笛儿，
唱吧，唱唱那快乐的小曲。”
于是我就唱，唱那首歌，
他听着，淌下了喜悦的泪滴。

“吹笛的人，坐下来写吧，
写成一本书，大家都能看。”

1. 指耶稣。

他刚说完，便隐去了形象，
我折下一根空心的芦管。

做出来一支土造水笔，
在笔中注满清清河水，
我用它写下快乐的歌谣，
孩子们都能高兴地听到。

牧羊人

牧人的好运多么美妙！
从早到晚他到处游荡；
他须整天跟随着羊群，
他的口中要充满颂扬——

他听到羔羊天真地叫，
他听到母羊纤柔地嚷；
他警觉着：它们安然无忧——
因为知道牧人就在近旁。

回音草坪

太阳升起，
使天空欢喜；
钟声欢鸣，
将春天欢迎；
云雀和鸫鸟，
灌木林中的小鸟，
到处高声唱——
和着欢欣的钟鸣；
我们就开始游戏
在那回音草坪。

满头白发的老约翰
无忧无虑地笑着，
坐在橡树下面，
坐在老人们中间；
他们笑我们嬉闹，
不久他们都说道：
“这样，这样作乐还是

当我们，全都年纪轻轻，
还是孩子时干的事，
在这回音草坪。”

直到小家伙们倦了，
再也提不起兴致；
太阳也落山了，
游戏才跟着完事。
妈妈们的裙兜周围，
围满了兄弟姐妹；
像鸟儿回到了窝里，
即将进入梦境；
看不到还有人游戏
在那渐黑的草坪。

羔羊

小羊羔儿，谁造了你？
你可知道是谁造了你？
给了你生命，吩咐你吃草，
在流水旁边，遍青青草地；
给了你人见人爱的衣裳，
茸茸的衣裳，鲜艳又柔软；
给了你那么柔和的声音，
让所有的溪谷听了都喜欢；
小羊羔儿，谁造了你？
你可知道是谁造了你？

小羊羔儿，我来告诉你，
小羊羔儿，我来告诉你：
他的名字和你的一样，
因为他叫自己羊羔羔儿；
他又柔顺，他又温和，
他变成了一个小小孩儿：
我是小孩儿，你是羊羔儿，

我们全都叫他的名儿。

　　小羊羔儿，上帝保佑你。

　　小羊羔儿，上帝保佑你。

黑人小孩

我妈妈生我在南方荒凉的地方，
我黑，可是啊！我的灵魂洁白；
白得像天使的是英国人的孩子，
可我黑，黑得好像失去了光彩。

在白昼的暑热中，妈妈坐着，
在一棵树下面她谆谆教导我；
她将我抱在膝上，把我亲吻，
她指着东方，开始对我诉说。

“看升起的太阳！那儿住着上帝，
他放射出光明，放射出热；
花草树木、飞禽走兽和人们
清晨得安慰，正午时分得欢乐。

“我们被安置在一块小小的天地，
我们可学着感受爱的光辉；
而这黑黑的肢体，晒黑的面容，
只是一片云，也像是多荫的树丛。

“当我们的灵魂学会忍受暑热，
那云会消散，他将召唤我们：
‘走出树林来吧，我的爱和担忧，
羔羊般快乐地围着我金色的帐篷。’”

妈妈亲着我，对我说了这些话。
我便这样对英国人的孩子谈讲：
当我从黑云[1]、他从白云[2]得到解放，
羔羊般快乐地围着上帝的篷帐，

我会为他遮阴，到他能忍受热，
能够快乐地倚着父亲[3]的膝盖；
我将站着，抚摸着他的银发，
变得像他一样，得到他的爱。

1. 指躯体。

2. 同上。

3. 指上帝。

鲜花

欢乐的欢乐的小雀，
在那么绿的叶子下面，
一朵幸福的花儿
见到你箭一样迅捷，
寻找你狭小的巢穴，
靠近我的心儿。

美丽的美丽的欧鸲，
在那么绿的叶子下面，
一朵幸福的花儿
听到你啜泣，啜泣，
美丽的美丽的欧鸲，
靠近我的心儿。

扫烟囱的孩子

我妈死去的时候我还很小，
我爸卖了我，那时我的小嘴
还叫不出“扫，扫，扫，扫”，
于是你的烟囱我扫，烟灰里我睡。

有个小汤姆长着羊毛般的鬈发，
剃光头时他哭得伤心，我就对他说：
“嘘，别介意，汤姆，光着头就知道
烟灰糟蹋不了你淡色的头发啦。”

他安静了下来。就在那天夜里，
汤姆在梦中见到这样的景象：
扫烟囱的孩子迪克、乔、小凯……
千万个全被关进黑洞洞的棺材。

后来，来了个带着亮钥匙的天使，
他打开棺材，让他们自由地离去，
他们穿过原野，跳呀，笑呀，
在清清河水中洗澡，在阳光中沐浴。

再光着白净的身子，扔了烟灰袋，
升上云端，在风中追逐游戏；
天使告诉汤姆，只要是好孩子，
就会有上帝做父亲，再不缺欢娱。

汤姆醒了，我们在黑暗中起身，
背着烟灰袋，拿起扫帚去干活。
早晨虽冷，汤姆却又暖和又愉快，
所以尽本分了，就不必怕受到伤害。

男童之失

“爸爸，爸爸，你去哪儿呀?
你别走这么快啊。
讲话呀爸爸，和你的儿讲话，
不然我会迷失啦。”

天黑了，哪里有什么爸爸。
孩子被露水沾湿了。
泥泞很深，孩子哭起来，
幻象也跟着消失了。

男童之得

小男孩迷失在孤寂的沼泽里，
向摇曳的灯光走去，
他哭着，但永在的上帝出现了，
像父亲，穿着白衣。

他吻了孩子，搀着他的手，
带领他去妈妈那里：
她正愁苦地在孤寂的山谷中
哭泣着找她的孩子。

笑歌

当绿色的树林以欢快的声音笑着，
那微波荡漾的流水笑着跑过，
当大气以我们的欢声笑语笑着，
绿色的山冈以它的喧声笑着，

当草地以它生动的绿色笑着，
蚱蜢在那欢乐的景象中笑着，
当玛丽，苏珊，还有爱弥丽她们
以甜蜜的小嘴唱着："哈哈——嗬！"

当色彩瑰丽的鸟儿在林荫中笑着，
放着樱桃和栗子的餐桌已摆开，
来住下吧，高高兴兴，和我一块儿，
齐声欢唱那悦耳的："哈哈——嗬！"

摇篮曲

甜蜜的梦儿，成一片暗影
罩在我可爱的婴儿头顶；
甜蜜地梦见怡人的流水，
借着幸福的静月的光辉。

甜蜜的睡眠，用柔软的绒羽
将你的眉编织成童稚花冠。
甜蜜的睡眠啊温柔的天使，
在幸福的孩儿上空盘旋。

甜蜜的微笑，在这夜间
在我的欢乐之上空盘旋；
甜蜜的微笑啊母亲的微笑，
哄走整个漫长的夜晚。

甜蜜的呻吟和温柔的叹息
不会驱走你眼中的睡意。
甜蜜的呻吟和更甜的微笑
哄走所有温柔的喁语。

睡吧，睡吧，幸福的孩子，
天地万物已微笑着安憩；
睡吧，睡吧，幸福地睡吧，
俯望着你，妈妈在哭泣。

甜蜜的宝贝，在你脸上
我能看到神圣的形象。
甜蜜的宝贝，曾经像你
造物主躺着，为我哭泣。

为我哭泣，为你，为全体，
那时他还是个小小的幼婴，
你永远看见他的形象——
超凡的面容微笑吟吟。

向你微笑，向我，向全体，
他变成过一个小小的幼婴，
童稚的微笑是他的真容，
将天国和尘世哄慰入静。

至上的形象

向仁慈、和平、怜悯与爱，
所有忧伤者恳切祈祷，
对这些蕴含着欢乐的美德，
他们以感激予以回报。

因仁慈、和平、怜悯与爱，
是上帝，我们亲爱的父，
仁慈、和平、怜悯与爱，
也是人——他的孩子和关注。

因为仁慈有一颗人心，
怜悯，有一张人的脸庞，
爱，有着至上的人形，
和平，有一套人的服装。

所以每一块地方每一个
处于忧伤之中的祈祷者，
都向至上的人形祈求
爱与仁慈与怜悯与和平。

所有人都应爱人的形象，

爱犹太人，土耳其人，土著，

它寓有仁慈与爱与怜悯，

上帝也在其中居住。

升天节

升天节到了，天真的脸蛋洗得干干净净，
孩子们一对对走着，穿着红黄绿各色衣裙，
灰发的助理牧师在前，执着雪一样白的手杖，
像泰晤士河水一样，他们流进了圣保罗大厅[1]。

这么一大群孩子啊！这些伦敦市的花朵！
他们神采奕奕，自动地结伴坐在一起，
一大群响着嗡嗡的声音，只是一大群羔羊哦，
无数男孩和女孩，举起了天真的手臂。

他们向天国扬起的歌声，就像劲风一样，
宛若天国的席位间悦耳的雷声飞驰。
他们后面是成年人——穷人贤明的保护者，
此刻你要心怀怜悯，免得从门前赶走天使。

---

1. 指圣保罗大教堂。

夜

夕阳沉落西山，
晚星闪耀在天上，
鸟儿在巢中安眠，
我也要将我的巢寻访。
月亮，像一朵花儿，
静静地怀着喜悦；
它安憩在高高的天庭，
对夜微笑吟吟。

别了啊，碧野和绿林，
这儿曾有欣欣
羊群，羔羊啃青，
欢快的天使脚步轻盈。
他们将欢乐和祝福
无形地不断倾注
在每朵鲜花和蓓蕾上，
在所有沉睡的胸上。

他们探遍不慎的鸟巢，
把鸟儿盖得和和暖暖；
他们访遍动物的洞穴，
使它们不受伤残；
他们若见谁哭泣，
谁就会熟睡过去——
洒睡眠于它们头上，
还坐在它们身旁。

当虎狼发出捕食的吼声，
他们就站住，哀然而泣——
试图驱散它们的渴望，
使它们免害群羊；
但它们若可怕地冲过去，
天使们就小心翼翼
接受每一个柔魂
去将新世界继承。

那里狮子红色的眼睛
将会流出金色的泪水，
并怜悯那些纤弱的呼叫，
漫步在羊群周围
说道："狂怒，被他的
柔顺；疾病，被他的
健康，驱逐出了
我们的永恒之世。

"在你身旁，咩咩的羔羊啊，
我现在能够躺下睡去；
或想着有你名字的他，
在后面吃草和哭泣——
经过生命河的洗礼，
我的闪亮的鬃毛
将永远闪耀如金，
当我守护着羊群。"

春

吹起长笛！

正当沉寂。

鸟儿嘻闹

白天夜里。

夜莺夜莺

溪谷中鸣，

云雀凌空，

欢乐地，

欢乐地，欢乐地，迎接新年。

小男孩儿

欢天喜地，

小女孩儿

可爱伶俐，

雄鸡欢叫，

你也欢叫。

欢乐之声，

童之喧声，
欢乐地，欢乐地，迎接新年。

小羔羊儿，
我在这儿，
过来舔舔
我雪白的脖儿，
让我拉拉
你柔软的毛儿，
让我亲亲
你柔软的脸儿，
欢乐地，欢乐地，我们迎接新年。

保姆之歌

当孩子们的声音从草坪传来，
欢笑声声飘荡在山冈，
我的心中就一片安宁，
周身都觉得宁静安详。

“该回来了，我的孩子，太阳下山了，
夜间的露水也已经出来；
得了，得了，快走吧，别玩了，
到明天天亮再来。”

“不，不，让我们玩嘛，还是白天呐，
我们一点也不想上床；
还有，小鸟儿还在天上飞翔，
满山遍野布满了绵羊。”

“唉，唉，去玩吧，玩到看不见了，
你们再回家睡觉去。”
小家伙跳啊，叫啊，笑啊，
山丘间回音四起。

童稚的欢乐

“我没有姓名，
出生只有两天。”
那我怎么叫你？
“我幸福欢欣，
欢乐是我的名。”
甜蜜的欢乐降给你！

美妙的欢乐！
甜蜜的欢乐才两天，
“甜蜜的欢乐”，我称你，
你甜甜地笑了，
我歌唱那一刻，
甜蜜的欢乐降给你！

一个梦

曾有一个梦编着树荫，
在我那天使守护的床顶；
我看见一只迷路的蚂蚁，
在我所躺的那片草地。

她苦恼，困惑，又孤凄，
夜色昏黑，她力尽精疲；
她翻过许多纠结的草茎，
我听到她心胆俱裂的声音：

“我的孩子啊！他们在哭泣？
他们可听到父亲在叹息？
他们一定四处去找我，
然后回去，为我哭泣。”

我流下了眼泪，为她哀恸；
但突然看到了一只萤火虫。
它应道：“是谁在哀哀地哭着，
哀哀地呼唤夜的巡察者？

“我是被派来照亮地面的，
还有甲虫在到处巡察；
好了，循着甲虫的声音，
小小迷路者，赶紧回家。”

对别人的悲伤

我会见到别人的苦恼
而不随之陷入伤悲？
我会见到别人的不幸
不为之寻求亲切的安慰？

我会见到滴落的泪珠
不感到在将悲伤分担？
会有父亲看到孩子
哭泣，不充满悲戚之感？

难道会有母亲坐视着
婴儿发出恐惧的呻吟？
不，不！永远不会，
永远，永远不会。

对一切都微笑的他[1]难道
会听到鹪鹩有一丝悲伤，

1. 指耶稣，耶稣投胎于圣母玛利亚腹内，变成了婴儿。

听到小鸟有不幸和烦恼，
听到婴儿忍受着苦恼，

而不坐在鸟巢旁边，
倾注同情于它们心里；
而不坐在摇篮旁边，
同婴儿眼泪流在一起；

而不日日夜夜地坐着，
将我们的眼泪全都擦去？
啊，不！永远不会，
永远，永远不会。

他将欢乐分给了全体，
他变成了一个小小的婴孩，
他变成了一个有苦恼的人，
他也感到了忧伤和悲哀。

别以为你有一次叹息
造物主他会不在前后，
别以为你有一次流泪
造物主他会不在左右。

啊！他[1]给了我们愉悦，
我们的悲伤他会消灭；
他总是坐在一旁叹息，
直等到我们的不幸离去。

1. 指造物主——上帝，与前面的“他”——耶稣并不矛盾，按“三位一体”之说，上帝为圣父，耶稣为圣子，为一体。

经验之歌

(1794)

序诗

听吟游诗人之声！

他看到现在、未来和过去，

他已听见

神明之言

漫步在古老的树林子里，

呼唤迷失的灵魂，

哭泣而涕下夜间的露水，

或许会操纵

北极明星

重新射出泯灭的光辉！

“地母啊，重现吧，地母！

请从露湿的草地上升起；

夜已消尽，

而那黎明

已从昏睡的氛围中升起。

"别再背转你的脸，
你为何还要把脸背过去？
星照的地面，
潮湿的海岸，
在破晓之前一直付与你。"

地母的回答

地母抬起了她的头，
从可怕而阴郁的黑暗之上。
她的光逃隐，
恐怖得寒心！
她的头发上是灰色的绝望。

“我囚于潮湿的海岸，
繁星的嫉妒使我的脏巢
寒冷又霉烂，
我泪水哭干
才听到古人的父亲[1]来到，

“因自私而善妒，胆怯，
人类的这个自私的父亲哟，
你用黑夜
链住欢悦，
少女和黎明怎能忍受？

1. 指上帝。

“春天藏起了欢乐吗，
在蓓蕾和鲜花生长的时候？
播种者在夜间
播种的吗？
耕犁者在暗中耕犁的吗？

“砸碎这沉重的锁链！
它僵住了我周身的筋骨，
自私！愚蠢！
永恒的毒根！
用奴役把自由的爱捆住。”

土块和卵石

“爱不图自己满意欢喜，
也不为自己小心留意，
却为了他人献出安逸，
在地狱的绝望中将天堂建起。”

一个小黏土块这样唱着，
被粘在牛脚上踏着踩着，
与一块溪中的卵石相遇，
它婉转地唱出这些韵律：

“爱只图自己满意欢喜，
强求于别人自己惬意，
取乐于他人失去安逸，
在天堂的憎恶中将地狱建起。”

升天节

难道这能算是至善，
在富饶多产的土地上——
婴儿的境遇悲惨，
被冰冷的放债的手喂养？

那嘶哭能算是歌声？
能算是欢乐的歌曲？
那么多孩子不幸啊，
那是块贫瘠的土地！——

那里见不着阳光，
土地荒芜不毛，
道路为荆棘所网，
冰雪四季不消。

哪里有了阳光，
哪里有雨露滋润，
婴儿就不会挨饿，
不会有令人心悸的贫困。

幼女之失

我预见
未来的大地
将从睡梦中
(请深深铭记)

起来和寻觅
她温顺的造物主：
荒原将变为
和暖的花园。

在那南国之疆，
那夏日之精华
永不凋谢的地方，
躺着可爱的丽卡。

我们可爱的丽卡，
好像已经过七夏；
她听着野鸟歌唱，
迷失的时间已很长。

“美丽的梦，快来吧，
我在这棵树的下面，
爸爸妈妈在哭吗——
哪儿丽卡能睡眠？

“你们幼小的孩儿，
已在荒原里迷路，
丽卡怎么能睡呢，
要是她妈妈在哭？

“要是妈妈心在痛，
就让丽卡醒着；
要是妈妈已安睡，
就不要让我伤悲。

“愁眉不展的夜啊，
快升起你的月吧，
在这莽莽荒原，
当我合上双眼。”

丽卡躺下睡了，
寻食的野兽来了，
从深深的大洞出来，
见到梦中的女孩。

那为王的狮子站着，
朝那处女看着；
然后来回地转，
在那片圣地上跳着。

虎豹围着她嬉戏，
学她躺着的姿势，
而那年老的狮子，
垂下金灿灿的鬃丝，

他的火眼含泪，
他舔着她的胸脯，
他的宝石般的泪水，
落在她的颈部。

于是那些个狮子，

为她解开了薄衣，

裸着梦中的少女，

把她抬往洞里。

幼女之得

丽卡的父亲和母亲，
整夜地悲痛伤心，
寻遍了深深的山谷，
荒野为他们悲哭。

他们疲惫又愁闷，
呻吟得哑了嗓门，
他们相依为命地
在荒原里摸索了七日。

七夜他们都睡在
浓浓的树荫里面，
梦见他们的女孩
饿死在荒原中间。

梦见她边哭边走，
在荒野中迷失了方向，
虚弱加上饥饿，
哭声嘶哑而凄凉。

睡不安只得起身，
那妇人直打哆嗦，
无奈凄惨的双脚，
乏得再不能往前挪。

他双臂将她抱紧，
一步一声悲叹，
一只狮子忽现，
正卧在他们路前。

回转去已是徒劳：
他用厚厚的鬃毛，
将他们掀倒在地，
又大步绕来绕去。

他嗅着他的猎物，
他们却稍稍胆壮；
他舔着他们的手，
静静地站在了一旁。

他们看他的眼睛，
感到无比地震惊：
他们惊奇地见到
一个金色的精灵。

他头上戴着王冠，
毛发从肩上披下；
他的毛发如金，
他们的忧虑消尽。

“跟我来吧，”他说道，
“别再为姑娘哭了，
在我的深宫里面
丽卡已安然入眠。”

那尤物前面走着，
他们在后面跟着，
他们见到孩子，
在猛虎中间躺着。

他们直到今天，

都住在孤寂的山谷，

既不怕狼的嚎叫，

也不惧狮子的咆哮。

扫烟囱的孩子

雪地里一个小黑点，
哭着“扫，扫”，叫人怜！
“你的爹妈在哪儿？说呀！”
“他们都去礼拜堂祈祷啦。

“我在荒野里曾经很快乐，
还在冬天的雪里欢笑，
他们就让我穿上黑衣，
叫我唱起悲伤的小调。

“我还是快乐，又跳又唱，
爹妈就以为没把我害够，
就去赞美上帝、神父和国王——
是他们在我们的苦难上建起天堂。”

保姆之歌

当孩子们的声音从草坪传来，
喁语阵阵轻飘在山谷，
我的春光就生动地浮现在脑海：
我的脸发青，一会儿又泛白。

该回来了，我的孩子，太阳落山了，
夜间的露水也已经出来，
你们的春光和白昼在游戏中荒废了，
你们的白昼和夜晚在借口中浪费了。

枯萎的玫瑰

玫瑰啊，你枯萎了！
飞行在黑夜里的
那无形的飞虫
在啸叫的风暴中

找到了你的
绯红色喜悦的床，
他的隐秘的爱情
毁了你的生命。

蝇

小小的蝇儿
你夏日的游戏
已被我的手
不慎拂去了。

难道我不是
你一样的蝇吗？
你不也是
我一样的人吗？

我喝酒跳舞，
唱唱歌曲，
直到盲目的手
擦伤我羽翼。

若思想是生命、
力量和呼吸，
而思想贫乏
就等于死去，

那我就是只
幸福的蝇，
不管我活着
还是死了。

天使

我做了个梦，它什么意思？
在梦中我是个未婚女王，
由一个温柔的天使守护：
愚蠢的悲哀，怎么也止不住！——

我日日夜夜不停地哭泣，
天使他替我擦去泪滴，
日日夜夜我不停地哭泣，
躲开他我才心中欢喜。

天使他拍起翅膀消失了，
黎明呈现出了玫瑰红，
我擦干眼泪，用十万盾矛
来压住我的惶惑惊恐。

不久，我的天使又来了，
我戒备着，他白来一趟——
我的青春已经消逝，
头上已是白发苍苍。

虎

虎，虎，光焰灼灼
燃烧在黑夜之林，
什么样的神手和神眼
构造出你可畏的匀称？

在海与天多深的地方，
燃着造你眼睛的火？
凭什么翅膀他敢追它，
凭什么手他敢捕捉？

凭什么肩膀，什么技艺，
才能拧成你的心肌？
何等可怖的手与脚才能
让你的心开始搏击？

用什么锤子，什么铁链，
在什么炉中将你的脑冶炼？
用什么砧子，何等铁手，
敢抓那令凡人致命的物件？

当天上的群星投下长矛，
用泪水浸湿了天空，
他在看着他的成果微笑？
是造耶稣的他将你创造？

虎，虎，光焰灼灼
燃烧在黑夜之林，
什么样的神手和神眼
构造出你可畏的匀称？

我美丽的玫瑰树

有人献给我一朵花儿，
一朵五月里见不到的花儿；
但我说“我有棵美丽的玫瑰树”，
我放弃了那朵可爱的花儿。

我走向我美丽的玫瑰树，
日日夜夜我将她照顾，
但是她疑忌地转过脸去，
她的刺成了我唯一的乐处。

太阳花

太阳花啊！厌倦了时间，
竟然数点起太阳的脚步，
寻找那美妙的金色所在，
漫游者结束旅程之处：

那里，因情欲而憔悴的青年，
和裹着冰雪的苍白的处女
却都从墓中起来，向往
我的太阳花想去的地方。

百合

羞怯的玫瑰竖着她的刺，
温驯的绵羊叉着吓人的角，
而洁白的百合会用怡人的爱——
不用刺也不用角，来点染她辉煌的美。

爱的花园

我来到爱的花园里面，
看到我从未见过的情形：
一座小教堂建在中央，
那儿原是我游戏的草坪。

这座小教堂大门紧闭，
门上写着“不许”的字样，
我于是转向爱的花园，
许多花曾在那儿吐送芬芳。

现在我看到的却是坟丘，
墓碑取代了昔日的花朵；
穿黑袍的神父来回转悠，
用刺蔷薇捆我的情欲和欢乐。

小流浪者

好妈妈，好妈妈，教堂里真冷，
酒吧里却惬意暖和又益身；
我习惯待着的还有别的地方，
那样的受用天堂里也比不上。

但若在礼拜堂能给我们点啤酒，
给一盆好火烤起我们的精神，
我们愿一辈子天天祷告歌唱，
一次也不想跑出去漂泊流浪。

牧师就可以讲道、喝酒和唱歌，
我们会像春天的小鸟一样快乐；
庄重的暗监夫人——她常在教堂，
就不会让罗圈腿的孩子挨打挨饿。

上帝会像一位父亲，高高兴兴，
看到孩子们跟自己同样地幸福，
再不会跟那个魔王或酒桶争吵，
而是亲吻他，给他酒又给他衣服。

伦敦

我走过每一条特辖大街，
附近特辖的泰晤士河在流淌，
我遇到的每一张脸上的痕迹，
都表露出虚弱，表露出哀伤。

在每个人的每一声呼叫之中，
在每个婴儿害怕的哭声里，
在一声一响，道道禁令中，
我听到精神之枷锁的碰击：

扫烟囱的孩子的哭叫多么
使每一个阴森的教堂惧怕，
还有那不幸的士兵的叹息
化成了鲜血从宫墙上淌下。

更不堪的是在夜半大街上
年轻妓女瘟疫般的诅咒，
它吞噬了新生婴儿的哭声，
将结婚喜榻变成了灵柩。

人之抽象

再也不会存在仁慈，
若大家像我们一样幸福；
同样也不会有怜悯存在，
如果不使有的人穷苦。

彼此间的恐惧产生和睦，
一直到自私的爱增长；
于是残忍就编织罗网，
细心地将诱饵播撒散布。

他怀着无比的敬畏坐下，
用他的泪水浇灌大地，
于是谦卑就在他脚下
伸出了它的虬结的根须。

不久他的头顶上方
蔓延开了神秘的暗影；
对于那些毛虫和苍蝇，
神秘正是它们的食粮。

它[1]终于结出欺诈之果，
红艳香甜，无比可口；
用它那浓密至极的树荫，
渡鸦[2]将自己的巢穴造就。

陆上和海里诸多神祇
寻遍自然寻找此树，
但他们全都是枉费辛苦：
人脑之中长着一株。

1. 指“谦卑”。

2. 可能指神父。

婴儿的悲伤

我妈妈呻吟！我爸爸哭泣，
我跳进了这个危险世界里。
赤条条无力自助，哭嚎着，
像魔鬼藏在一片阴影里。

在我爸爸手中挣扎着，
跟我的襁褓拼命反抗着，
又被裹着，又累，我只想
在我妈妈的乳房上解气。

有毒的树

我对朋友愤怒，
我表明愤怒，怒气就没了；
我对敌人愤怒，
我不予表露，这怒气长着。

我提心吊胆将它浇灌，
日夜浇灌着泪滴；
我用微笑来将它照耀，
用软软的狡诈的诡计。

它日日夜夜地生长，
终于结出了鲜亮的苹果；
我的敌人看到它闪光，
他知道那苹果属于我。

当夜色将树身遮掩，
他就溜进园子里偷食：
早晨我高兴地看到
我的敌人在树下挺尸。

少年之失

“没有人爱别人像爱自己，
也谈不上那样尊重别人，
比思想本身知道得更多，
对思想来说也不可能。

“父亲[1]啊，我怎能更加爱你，
或者更爱我的兄弟？
我爱你就像小小的鸟雀，
在门前啄食面包的碎屑。”

神父坐在他旁边谛听，
激动地抓住他的头发：
他拽着小外衣揪牢这孩子，
大家都佩服他神父的心机。

他站在高高的祭坛之上：
“瞧，这儿有个恶魔！”

1. 指上帝。

他说："他竟捏造出论据
来指责我们最神圣的神秘。"

听不见哭着的孩子的声音，
哭着的双亲枉然地哭泣；
他被剥得只剩件小衬衣，
被人用一根铁链子捆起。

在一处圣地他被焚烧，
从前那儿焚烧过多人，
哭着的双亲枉然地哭泣，
这种事阿尔比恩[1]海岸有吗？

1. 英格兰的古称。

少女之失

未来时代的孩子们
读着这愤慨的一页，
会知道从前的时候，
爱！甜蜜的爱！被当作罪孽。

在那黄金时代，
没有冬天的寒冷，
欢快的青年男女，
于神圣的灯[1]下
在和煦的光中裸着游戏。

曾有对青年男女，
充满了柔情蜜意，
相会在明亮的花园，
当神圣的灯，
刚刚拉去那夜的幕帘。

1. 指太阳。

升起的曙光之中
他们在草地上游戏；
父母们不在近前，
陌生人远离此地，
不久姑娘就忘记了恐惧。

亲够了甜蜜的吻，
他们约定要重逢，
在那安谧的睡梦
飘拂过深空，
而疲惫的旅人悲叹的时辰。

善意的父亲跟前，
来了欢快的少女；
但他那疼爱的神色
就像圣经一般，
她害怕得娇躯抖抖瑟瑟。

“欧娜！你脸色苍白！
快对你父亲坦白，
真让人心儿发抖！
哦，忧愁啊，
真要把我的灰发愁白！”

致特拉[1]

出身于凡胎的芸芸众生，
都将毁灭，消失躯体。
摆脱生殖而自由地复活：
那我何必和你在一起？

男女们出生于羞耻和骄傲，
在早晨开花，在黄昏死去；
但仁慈令死亡变成了安眠，
男女们复活了，激动哭泣。

你，我的凡体的母亲，
用残忍套住了我的心灵，
用那欺人又自欺的眼泪，
裹住我的鼻耳和眼睛：

用无知的泥土堵住我嘴，
使我背叛了尘世的生命；

1. 不详。可能指下文“我的凡体的母亲”。

耶稣之死使我无羁：[1]

那我何必和你在一起？

1. 这是一个灵魂的复活。——原注

小学生

我爱在夏天的清晨起床，
当鸟儿鸣啭在棵棵树上；
猎人远远地吹着号角，
云雀儿伴我歌唱，
啊！多美妙的伙伴。

但要在夏天的清晨上学，
唉！这把兴致都扫尽；
在那严厉昏花的眼底，
小同学们垂头丧气地
把一天苦熬过去。

唉！我有时得颓丧地坐着，
度过许多个急人的钟点，
我得不到快乐，无论从书中
或是和一帮无聊的讨厌鬼
同坐在书斋里挨时间。

为了欢乐而出世的鸟儿
怎能坐在笼中歌唱?
孩子怎能一受惊扰就
垂下他娇嫩的翅膀,
忘记了朝气蓬勃的春天?

爸爸妈妈啊，若花蕾被摘,
花儿被刮落在地,
若是嫩弱的幼苗被悲哀
和满腹的重重心事夺去
他们春天里的欢愉,

夏天怎么会高兴地露头,
夏天的果实怎么会露脸?
怎收拾悲伤所毁的一切,
如何祝福丰美的一年,
当冬天的狂风出现?

古代吟游诗人之声

到这里来吧，快乐的年轻人，
看这展布着的黎明，
真理新生的象征。
疑惑消失了，及理性的阴影，
及无知的争辩和狡猾的戏弄。
愚蠢是一条无尽的迷途，
纠结的根蔓困着她的路，
多少人在那里绊倒！
他们整夜在尸骨上跌蹶，
却自认为想知道的无不知晓，
他们需要引导，却好为人师。

至上的形象

残忍据有人的心灵；
嫉妒据有人的脸庞；
恐怖据有至上的人形，
隐秘据有人的服装。

人的服装是锻过的铁器，
人的外形是熊熊的锻炉，
人的脸庞是封闭的熔炉，
人心是它的饥饿的胃部。

内心旅行者

我途经一个男人的国度，
这国度里有男人也有女人；
我所见闻的骇人的事情，
乃冷漠的尘世旅行者所未闻。

那里的婴儿出生于欢乐，
然而受孕于不幸的伤悲；
正如我们欢乐地收割，
播种时却洒下悲酸之泪。

如果那婴儿生而为男，
他就被交给一个老妇，
她将他钉在石头上面，
用金杯接他那尖声的嚎哭。

她用铁蒺藜捆住他的手，
她将他的手和脚全刺穿，
她割下他的心放在旁边，
让它对热与冷都有所体验。

她的手把每根神经都数过，
就像吝啬鬼查点黄金；
她靠他的哭嚎生活：
他愈益年长，她愈益年轻。

最后他变成个流血的青年，
她则变成了鲜艳的处女，
然后他将他的手铐砸烂，
为了取乐将她捆起。

他用她全部的神经来育己，
像丈夫种他的模型一般；
她变成了他的居住之地
和一个七十倍丰产的果园。

他很快衰老成老年的影子，
绕着尘世的小屋踱步，
他身上装满黄金和宝石，
那是他勤劳所致的财富。

这是人类灵魂的宝石，
是相思的眼睛里的珍珠和红玉，
是痛苦的心灵中的无数金子，
是殉难者的呻吟和情人的叹息。

这是他的食物和饮料；
他以此款待穷人和乞丐，
款待徒步旅行的旅人：
他的门永远对他们敞开。

他的苦是他们永恒的欢乐；
他们使屋顶和墙壁唱歌；
直到荒原上的野火之中
出生了一个女性的婴儿。

她整个身体是固体的火焰、
宝石和黄金。婴儿的身体
他不敢伸手抚摸，也不敢
将她包裹在襁褓里面。

但她找来了她所爱的男人，
不管穷或富，青年或老年；
他们很快驱逐了年老的主人，
让他行乞于他人的门前。

他流着泪漂泊，走向远方，
最后他被人收留供养，
他又老又驼、浑身痛、眼睛瞎，
最后他赢得了一位姑娘。

为了减轻他冻僵的年纪，
这可怜人将她抱在怀里，
小屋在他面前渐渐凋敝，
花园也失去了可爱的魅力。

变化的景色改变了一切，
于是旅客遍布于九州；
感官恐惧地到处乱滚，
平坦的大地变成了圆球。

日月星辰，全部消隐，
荒原茫茫，无边也无沿，
食物没有了，水也没有，
四周全是茫茫的荒原。

她的微笑里面的面包，
她的稚嫩双唇上的甘蜜，
她流盼的眼睛里任性的游戏，
将他哄向婴儿时期。

因为他每天又吃又喝，
所以他变得愈益年轻；
在荒野上面，他们两个
恐惧而沮丧地四处漂零。

她像野鹿一样地逃走，
用恐惧种下了许多野灌木丛；
他追赶着她，日夜不休，
被各种爱情的艺术所诓哄。

他受骗于各种爱和恨的艺术，
终于，在广阔的荒野上面
布满了任性的爱情的迷宫，
野猪、狮和狼漫游其间。

终于，她变成个哭泣的老妇，
他则变成了任性的婴儿，
太阳和星辰更近地运转着，
许多的情侣漫游到这儿。

树上结出了甜蜜的狂喜，
奉给荒野的每一位游客；
终于建起了许多城市，
许多牧人的快乐的家舍。

可他们发现了那皱眉的婴儿，
整个地区被恐怖所笼罩，
“那个婴儿！婴儿出生了！”
他们逃了，连滚带跑。

因为谁敢摸那皱眉的形象，
手臂就会枯萎无遗；
野猪和狮狼齐吼着奔逃，
每棵树木都凋落了果实。

除非那人是一个老妇，
没人敢摸那皱眉的形象；
她将他钉在石头上面，
诸事完毕，如我叙说过的那样。

译者说明

此译本内容皆选自我 1981 年至 1983 年初所译《布莱克诗集》。此前该诗集已出版过三个版本：上海三联书店 1999 年版、台湾书林出版有限公司 2007 年英汉对照版(《布雷克诗选》) 和上海社会科学院出版社 2017 年版。

该诗集译自 *William Blake's Poems and Prophecies* (Everyman's Library, 1927)，并参照 *Selected Poems of William Blake* (Oxford University, 1957) ; *The Poetical Works of William Blake* (Oxford University, 1913) ; *Blake's Poetry and Designs* (W. W. Norton & Company, 1979)。

在很长一段时间里，布莱克的诗作大部分是以手稿形式存世的，后英美多家出版社在出版时各自进行了整理和

校勘，所以各版本之间互有不同。为此，译者今依照企鹅兰登版的英文，对译文做了些许相应的改动。

张炽恒

2018 年 3 月 18 日于上海

企鹅经典：小黑书　第一辑

01. 贝尔科洛蕾夫人与神父
[意] 薄伽丘

02. 泄密的心
[美] 爱伦·坡

03. 醋栗
[俄] 契诃夫

04. 一个人需要许多土地吗?
[俄] 列夫·托尔斯泰

05. 一颗简单的心
[法] 福楼拜

06. 傻子的一生
[日] 芥川龙之介

07. 萎缩的胳膊
[英] 托马斯·哈代

08. 樱花树下的清酒
[日] 吉田兼好

09. 虎！虎！
[英] 威廉·布莱克

10. 给一个青年诗人的十封信
[奥] 里尔克